S,

OCCU͏ ͏ ͏ ͏ ͏ ͏ ͏ ͏ ͏ ͏ ͏ ͏ ͏ ͏

GW01003274

ALL HALLOWS' EVE

BRON JAMES

www.bronjames.co.uk
www.samhainscasebook.co.uk

The *Sam Hain* series was first dreamt up as a Halloween story for All Hallows' Read. This book is the first of that series.

All Hallows' Read is the tradition of giving the gift of supernatural and scary books around the time of Halloween, started by acclaimed author Neil Gaiman.

SAM HAIN
ALL HALLOWS' EVE

The Veil between Worlds thins this Night,
Giving rise to things both Dark and Light.

CHAPTER I

That Halloween had started out just like any other. The annual after-work costume party kicked off early in the evening, rapidly descending into an alcohol-fuelled frenzy as inebriated skeletons and zombies danced the night away, while the vampires tried desperately to get off with the scantily clad nurses. The other drunken denizens of the night, those who had come dressed as something other than the undead – like the inside-joke costumes and the mock-costume of Geoff from Admin – sat in the corner, explaining to one another the inspiration for their outfits and exactly why it's supposed to be funny.

Unlike previous Halloweens, Alice Carroll had decided to leave the party early. The turning point for her had come somewhere between King Kong throwing up on her shoes and most of the party-goers spontaneously deciding to go trick-or-treating at one o'clock in the morning. In the East End of London. As far as brilliant ideas were concerned, this was not one of them. Alice could not see a group of drunk Halloween caricatures knocking on people's doors in the small hours of the morning turning out well.

Having rinsed the last of King Kong's vomit from her formerly bright yellow shoes in the kitchen sink, Alice brushed back her blonde hair and put the comically springy antennae of her sexy bee costume back on her head. Throwing her denim jacket around her shoulders, she took her leave.

She'd managed to leave the party with very little hassle. Alice had let Rachel, her flatmate, know she was going to start heading home, to which Rachel had responded with an 'aw, no, you should stay!' before drunkenly dancing off in the direction of Frankenstein's Monster. Other than that, everyone else seemed too wrapped up in their night to notice the girl in the yellow-and-black striped corset leaving. Alice walked through the crowded hallway, pushing through groups of chattering ghosts and werewolves, squeezing past the wholly unsettling sight of Marilyn Monroe making out with the Creature from the Black Lagoon, and slipped out of the door and started walking down the road. She was thankful she didn't have to keep explaining she was leaving to everyone she passed, but it did feel a little surreal going straight from the packed house party to the quiet of the streets without really saying goodbye to anyone.

The walk home was an old and familiar one. Alice had moved to Islington scarcely a year ago, but she had already found the roads that made her feel most at home. Her favourite part of the walk home was up through an old street just off of the main road. It was the kind of old, side-alley kind of street that would host a farmers market on Wednesdays and an antiques fair over the weekend, and had a distinctly quaint, Old London feel to it. It felt like a small bubble in the city, separated from the rest of metropolis, and seemed perpetually stuck in the past.

For Alice, it was a homely street. It was where she occasionally bought fresh vegetables mid-week and where one weekend she had bought an old mantel clock for a fiver, only to discover upon getting it home that it didn't work. However, this night, on Halloween, in the cold of winter, when no other person was about – save for the roaming parties patrolling the main road an alley or two away – there was something eerie about this old cobbled street. Alice's every footstep echoed off of the aged, soot-covered brickwork. In the distance, she could hear the noise of those continuing their pub crawls out on the main road, and that distant sound of the crowd made her feel safe, yet vulnerable too.

She walked through the empty streets back to her flat, boggle-eyed springy antennae bouncing annoyingly as she went. The sexy bee costume had been a dare, a forfeit for having to work a slightly longer shift and turn up late to the party. It had never really occurred to Alice exactly why the sexy bee costume existed; it wasn't the most intuitive of sexy costumes. Most bee drones lived out their entire lives as virgins, and queen bees were hardly renowned for being sensual lovers. And honey bees leave their sting behind in whomever they've just stung, ripping out most of their internal organs in the process, leaving them to die a slow and painful death. In fact, Alice thought, there was very little that was traditionally sexy about bees. It also wasn't the best choice of costume for walking home on a cold winter's night, but here she was in the stripy corset and black lace tutu, walking the cold, dark streets of Islington.

Maybe it was the in-depth thoughts she was having about bee costumes, or the mild detachment from reality caused by more jellied-vodka eyeballs than she'd care to count, but Alice had failed to notice that she was being followed. A short distance behind her walked a man, hunched over, his head low and a hood pulled down over his face, shambling his way along the cobbled street. He stumbled on the uneven road, and stopped in his tracks when Alice eventually turned to look at him. The man stood eerily still, like a waxwork come to life, and although she couldn't see his eyes, she could feel him watching her. The noise from the nearby main road had fallen silent, as if everyone had suddenly decided to call it a night, and a haunting quietness hung heavily in the air. It was as if the world had abruptly ground to a halt. There wasn't even the faintest whisper of a breeze. The night was perfectly still.

Alice carried on walking at a slightly faster pace. She was a good five minutes walk from home, but she really didn't fancy being in the street with this man for too much longer. One of the street lamps ahead of her flickered uncertainly.

She could hear his footsteps behind her, uneven and clumsy, but gradually speeding up. His footsteps matched hers. She didn't want to provoke anything by breaking into a run, but she quickened her pace. She continued to walk faster and faster, almost approaching a light jog. The man sped up also, and Alice could feel her heart pumping rapidly in her throat.

Suddenly, something slammed into her. She was pushed to the wall of the street in one whirlwind motion, winding her as she hit the hard brick surface. The force that had pushed her moved away, and she turned around, staggering and dazed from the impact. As she struggled to regain her balance, she saw the man who had been walking behind her charge past at full pelt and come to an abrupt stop. He turned slowly, unnaturally, and out of the corner of her eye she caught a glimpse of another person. A tall figure silhouetted against the orange glow of the street lamps, dressed from head to toe in black, a greatcoat flowing down to his ankles, and a fedora-style hat perched on his head.

'Run!' The silhouetted figure shouted, gesturing towards one of the nearby side-streets. Alice stood for a moment, dumb-founded, and watched as this other man squared up to her initial pursuer. The hooded man moved towards them, slowly, purposefully, and his head juddered unnaturally. For a brief second, the street lamps dimmed, leaving the alleyway in darkness. With a buzzing sound, the lights struggled back on. The man in the coat and hat turned to her again and waved his arm frantically in the direction of the street. 'Go!'

She didn't think to question the man's orders. She ran. The bee antennae bobbed up and down irritatingly in front of her face as she sprinted away. She didn't stop to catch her breath as she ran, and even sacrificed one of her shoes to the night as she continued to sprint as fast as she could through the winding alleyways. Behind her, Alice heard a loud zap and the crackling of electricity, and she turned to see the street behind her illuminated by a bright purple flickering light. She squinted at the bright light for a second, and carried on running in the opposite direction, away from whatever that was, and, unwittingly, away from home. She had not been down these roads before and, in her panic and confusion, she had lost all sense of direction.

Rounding a corner, she slowed her pace to a jog and eventually came to a stop. She leaned against a wall, struggling to catch her breath as a mix of panic and exhaustion overwhelmed her. Looking around, Alice tried to get her bearings. She was in a back-alley, the narrow street lined with old, scorched brick walls, and every few feet sat small piles of black bags. The way was lit by only a few dimly glowing street lamps, giving everything a gentle orange hue. Alice reached into her pocket and pulled out her phone, fumbling with the screen-lock as she tried to calm her sudden rush of nerves. She flicked her way through the pages of apps and prodded at the Maps icon impatiently, desperately hoping the

GPS could tell her what road she was now on.

Location settings disabled. Insufficient data.

'Shit,' Alice muttered under her breath. She tried calling Rachel, but it didn't matter where she stood, there was no signal. She sighed in frustration, and shoved the phone back into her jacket pocket.

As Alice stood there, perplexed and alone and more than a little bit frightened, a tall figure loomed out of one of the pitch black alleyways and stepped into the dim, orangey-yellow glow of the street lamps. She let out a slight whimper when she caught sight of the ominous silhouette. The figure stood for a moment, and she recognised the shape of the coat and hat in the low light.

'Sorry about that,' the figure spoke in a calm and friendly voice, the greatcoat billowing out behind him as he made his way forward. As he came closer, Alice knew for certain it was the man from a few moments before, and although it seemed like it would be a good idea, she didn't feel compelled to start running again. The man leaned against the wall next to her. 'Are you okay?'

'Really? Do you *think* I'm okay?' Alice immediately exclaimed, staring almost accusingly at the man. 'I've been followed home by some creepy guy, been pushed into a wall, run from a fight, I've had King Kong throw up on my shoes – one of which is now missing – I'm cold, I'm tired, I'm dressed like a slutty bee, and I don't know where I am any more. Am I okay?! You bloody tell me!' Most of Alice's fear and panic had converted itself into anger. She just wanted to get home and be done with the night.

The man simply looked deep into her eyes, and smiled kindly at her. 'I'm sorry you had to experience all that,' he said, far too calmly for Alice's liking, 'these kind of things, they shouldn't happen. Difficult to keep on top of it all at this time of year, of course.'

She glared at him, and got the first proper look at the man since he'd rather abruptly slammed her into the wall. He must have been in his mid-to-late-twenties, possibly early thirties, and a little over six foot tall. His scruffy, mid-length dark brown hair flowed out from under his hat and rested on the upturned collars of his overcoat. A silver talisman, a five-pointed star inside a circle, hung from a cord around his neck and rested on his chest. It looked as if he'd decided to dress as a contemporary Van Helsing for Halloween.

'What? What are you talking about? What was all that back there, and who the hell are you?!' Alice asked, still on the offensive. 'And what about the other guy?!'

'One question at a time,' the man said wearily. 'First of all, that was something which crossed the threshold from another world and into this one. I came to send it back.' Alice simply stood staring at him, incredulous. He continued. 'This is one of those strange supernatural stories people read about online or in Esoteric Express. Most people dismiss these stories as myths, rumours or hoaxes,' he chuckled, 'if only they knew.' He was incredibly matter-of-fact about the whole affair, and Alice couldn't help but wonder if this was all some kind of elaborate Halloween joke.

'It's gone now, though. Back to the Void space where it belongs. At this time of year, the veil between worlds is incredibly thin; easier for them to cross the threshold, but easier for me to send them back, too.' He straightened his lapels with the air of a man congratulating himself on a job well done.

Alice stood silently for a while, just staring at this man, taking in everything he was saying, but refusing to believe a word of it. She shook her head, and with a sarcastic 'yeah, right!' she began to hobble away. She took off her remaining shoe to even herself out. She'd had more than enough of this evening, and wasn't going to put up with much more of this nonsense. She just wanted to go home.

'No, you're quite right. It's all rather hard to believe. Too far-fetched,' he retorted, and tipped his hat in her direction. 'Have a good evening.'

Alice turned to give him a snarky response – her evening had been far from good – but he had vanished. It was as if he'd evaporated into thin air. *I've definitely had enough of this evening*, she concluded, and scurried back the way she'd come, hoping to find her way back to somewhere she recognised. It didn't take long for her to find somewhere vaguely familiar, and once she'd got her bearings, she headed straight for home.

Almost falling through the door to her flat, Alice stumbled in, overcome with stress and fatigue and alcohol, and she unceremoniously flopped herself onto the sofa. She had barely taken the ridiculous bee antennae off of her head before she fell asleep and drifted off into a strange and uneasy night's dreaming.

That night, her dreams were haunted by strange visions. Visions of tall men in overcoats fighting demons in hooded jackets; of a giant gorilla climbing the Empire State building with a yellow-and-black striped shoe; and of bees with weirdly cartoon-y eyes on springs, dancing seductively. It was not the best night's sleep she'd ever had by any means.

CHAPTER II

Alice woke up the next morning with the hangover from hell. It was the kind of hangover that felt like goblins had crept in during the night and had decided that her head would make the perfect addition to their percussive band. She briefly panicked when she attempted to get up from the sofa and caught sight of the clock. *Half-past ten? I'm late!* She staggered to her feet, tried to keep her balance, and then remembered she'd moved her shift to the afternoon, pre-empting this very morning. And just as well, too. The world was a terrifyingly spinny and throbby place that morning, and Alice resolved – much like she did after every night out – never to drink again.

At first, there was very little she could piece together of the night before, only fragments of events and what felt like the weird fever-dreams that only a certain amount of vodka could produce. *Geoff had been there... Or was it Tim, dressed as Geoff? Dracula was doing a little more than sucking the blood from the neck of Nurse Naughty. Someone had come dressed as King Kong, too.*

She balanced herself as the world took another sickening spin, placing her hand on the back of the sofa to stay upright, and she hobbled into the kitchen. She had lost a shoe at some point, that was certain. Her feet felt cold and blistered. Pouring more than a generous amount of coffee granules into a mug, Alice put the kettle on and gazed vacantly into the fridge. *Something fried will do*, she thought, *like fried eggs in a sandwich. With bacon. And loads of ketchup poured on top.* She set about preparing her decadent cure, poured herself a coffee strong enough to raise the dead, and decided to lie back down while she waited for the bacon and eggs to fry.

Van Helsing was also there last night, she seemed to recall. Although that seemed more distant than other parts of the evening. Maybe an odd dream. She thought she could remember Van Helsing beating up a hoody, but that seemed more like it would fit in with her strange night's sleep rather than the Halloween party. She pushed all thoughts of the night before aside. She'd have breakfast, wake up properly, boot the hangover and clear her head, go to work and get on with her day.

The breakfast she'd prescribed herself did just the job. The strong, bitter coffee scared off the fuzziness in her brain, and the sandwich, dripping with grease and ketchup and packed so full with eggs and bacon she had to open her mouth as wide as she could just to take a bite, seemed to help stabilise her body for the day ahead. She still felt a little fuzzy, but at least the pounding headache was starting to ease off and she didn't feel half as nauseated as she did before.

Alice made her way into the bathroom, and splashed her face with a handful of cold water. It was a refreshing sensation, and she rubbed her eyes to clear the tiredness. Leaning against the sink, she let out a quiet groan. It was going to take more than coffee, fried sandwiches, and cold water to completely shift this hangover.

As she looked up into the mirror, Alice was suddenly shaken to the core, and all colour drained from her face. There, stood immediately behind her and staring back at her from the reflection, was the hooded man from the night before. She wheeled around to face him, wide eyed and much more alert than she thought she was capable of being, but suddenly he was nowhere to be seen. The bathroom was empty. She turned back to the mirror, and all she could see was herself reflected in its surface, the bath and toiletry cabinet the only things behind her.

Adrenaline pumped through her body, and she let out a deep, panicked breath. Steeling herself, Alice walked slowly, cautiously, towards the bath. The shower curtain was drawn half-way across, and with a tentative shaking hand she reached out to pull it away. With a swift flick of her wrist, Alice whipped the curtain across, pulling it open in a flash

A single sad droplet of water dripped from the end of the tap.

Alice breathed a sigh of relief, and returned to the living room. Settling back down on the sofa, she checked the clock, and told herself she'd nap for a little bit to digest breakfast and finish off the hangover. She tried to push all thoughts of last night's misadventures and nightmares aside, thinking that once she'd had a bit more sleep she'd forget all about it.

Of course, she did not forget.

As she tried to sleep, her mind was flooded with strange visions from the night before. It wasn't quite like a dream, but definitely not reality. She could see the old cobbled street and the hooded man as vividly as if she was there, but it also felt distant and dream-like. She was still aware she was just sprawled out on her sofa, but there was something incredibly tangible about this strange, waking dream. She was running down the street, her legs pounding and lungs tight as she tried to breathe and she knew that if she stopped, even for a second, he would catch up with her. The street stretched out before her, growing longer and longer as she ran until eventually it felt like she was going nowhere at all. Her legs ached and began to weaken and wobble as she kept running. Tentatively glancing behind her, Alice could see the hooded man standing right behind her, and no matter how fast she tried to run, she couldn't move from that spot. The hidden face of the man leered forwards.

'*Tenebris venit*,' he breathed down the back of her neck. She felt shivers run down her spine and her skin turned cold.

BANG! Alice woke from the dream with a

start, sitting bolt upright and breathing heavily. It took a while for her to compose herself and gather her bearings, but she realised she was home and safe, woken by the noise of the flat's letterbox. She turned to see the letterbox still flapping slightly, creaking on its hinges as it slowly swung back and forth, but no post had been delivered.

The nightmare felt like it had lasted forever, but when she checked her phone, she saw she'd only been asleep for half an hour. Reaching for her mug, she drank the last gulp of the grainy – now cold – coffee and grimaced. Today was going to be a difficult day.

Alice tried to push the strange thoughts to the side while she focussed on getting ready for work. She showered, put on something a bit more suitable for work than the corset and tutu of the bee costume, and started to do her make-up. She had half considered talking to Rachel about her nightmare, just for reassurance that she needn't worry, but when her flatmate came staggering through the door shortly after noon, clutching a bottle of schnapps shouting 'woo, hair of the dog!' she thought better of it. Rachel slammed the door behind her, making Alice's brain shake.

'Please, don't,' Alice said, clutching one hand to her still-hungover head, 'not so loud.' Rachel bounced over to the sofa and sat down next to her.

'You need some of this in you, then,' Rachel said, holding the bottle of schnapps out. Alice took a quick swig and made a 'nope' face.

'Ew, no, bad plan. I feel bad enough as it is.'

'How?! You didn't have that much last night, and you walked home. I don't feel that bad!'

'Maybe because you carried on drinking.'

'True,' Rachel said, and she took another swig from the bottle, 'how'd you get home last night, anyway?'

Flashes of the street, of the man in the hood and then of the man in the coat and hat, ran through Alice's mind. She thought about the ache in her legs as she ran, the panic tight in her chest, and losing a shoe somewhere along the line. Then she remembered the bright purple flash, and the strange things the man had said to her.

'There was a fight down the alley on my way back, and I think someone was following me for a while. I don't know, I was very drunk, it's all a bit of a mess.'

'Are you okay?' Rachel asked, putting a hand on Alice's knee sympathetically.

'Yeah. Yeah! I'm fine. Just a bit of a bad night really.'

'Not still going to work, are you? I've called in sick, me.'

'Yeah, I am,' Alice said dejectedly as she reached for her hairbrush and quickly ran it through her hair. She stood up and glanced around, looking for her shoes.

'No, stay home! We can watch films and order takeaway and wallow in hungover self-pity.'

'As fun as that sounds, I really can't afford to

take the day off, Rachel. My manager was bad enough when I asked to move my hours to the afternoon, let alone if I don't go in at all.'

'Oh, you're no fun,' Rachel said teasingly. 'Tonight, though. Pizza, cider, chick-flicks, the works.'

'Fine! You've twisted my arm,' Alice said with a smile, 'Friday night in. Sounds good. Just what I need.'

Rachel nodded in sagely agreement. 'You're overworked and spend your time worrying about silly things-'

'Like the rent?' Alice interrupted.

'You know what I mean. You're always stressing about something or another. You need to take some time to chill, babe.'

This time it was Alice's turn to nod sagely. 'Yeah, you're right,' she said, 'I've not been taking much time for myself. Maybe I am just overstressed.' She had been running herself into the ground with work just to try and keep a roof over her head, but it hardly gave her a sense of self. She was simply Server #0, working on the shop floor for eight hours a day, and receiving more abuse from customers and staff alike than she really believed was possible.

'Perfect! It's what we both need to relax,' Rachel said. 'And whatever's on your mind, I'll try to take it off of you.'

'Thank you. But first, work,' Alice declared. She threw her coat around her shoulders, wrapped her scarf tightly around her neck, and pulled her bobble hat on. 'I'll see you tonight,' she said with a wave, and left the flat.

The weather outside was bitterly cold that afternoon. It was the kind of weather that was equal parts refreshing and misery-inducing, and Alice was more inclined to feel the latter. She sat huddled on the crowded tube carriage on the way to work, nestled under her thick, woollen coat and wearing more layers than she could count. Her scarf was tightly wrapped up around her neck, and pulled up to cover her nose from the cold. She much preferred the summer. At least it was warmer on the underground than it had been outside, even if the air was a little dusty.

The journey to work always made Alice feel miserable, always dreading stepping off of the tube and walking around the corner to the store where she worked. Day in, day out, she'd fall into the usual routine, sat on a claustrophobic and increasingly packed train on the way to work, where all she did was stand behind the tills, serving customers and packing their bags, likely getting shouted at because she wasn't folding their shirts quite right, or receiving disgruntled remarks whenever she had to direct someone to customer services. Then she'd likely make fewer sales than her co-workers and be told to 'up her game if you want to make it in retail,' which, of course, she did not. Same old, same old.

The tube had been stopping and starting from

the minute they pulled out of Highbury and Islington station, something to do with signal failures on the Victoria line, and Alice was starting to worry that she'd be late. She may not have wanted to go into work, but nor did she want to announce her lateness after management had already picked her up for clocking in ten minutes late because of a tube delay in the past. She glanced at the time on her phone. *Not too late yet*, she thought, *I should have five minutes to get there from the station*. As if to mock her optimistic outlook on time, the train came to a grinding halt again. Sparks flew up outside of the window, briefly illuminating the normally unseen passages of the London Underground. A number of men in suits tutted with world-weary irritation as the tube came to a full stop.

'We apologise for the delay,' a voice came crackling through the tannoy, 'but due to a signalling issue at Warren Street Station, we will have to wait here for approximately five minutes.'

Alice rolled her eyes. *Just typical*.

The glare of the fluorescent lights above the passengers' heads began to flicker, and the carriage started to grow dimmer and dimmer. Then, with a unified buzzing noise, the lights went out, plunging the carriage into darkness. Alice looked around nervously, she was uncomfortable on the underground at the best of times, let alone when sat in pitch blackness, stuck in a tunnel with no way out. She could just about make out the outlines of her fellow passengers, some of whom were still trying to read the Metro in spite of the absence of light. It was then that she noticed the person sat opposite her. He was hunched over, his head facing the floor, and his features covered by his hood. She felt a shiver as she recognised the unearthly air about the figure, but it couldn't possibly be... *Could it?* She wondered, staring at the all too familiar clothing.

As she stared at the man, trying to convince herself it wasn't her nightmarish apparition, his head slowly began to rise. The lights flickered back on for only a moment, and she saw him staring back at her with haunting, unblinking eyes. But they weren't really eyes. Where eyes should have been there were two almond-shaped black holes. They didn't look so much like holes into the head, but holes torn in the fabric of reality, and it wasn't really a blackness as much as it was... Nothingness. Alice froze in fear, unable to break her eye-contact with this thing that seemed to have manifested itself from her nightmares. She was too afraid to blink, and she could feel the man staring into her soul with his unseeing, non-existent eyes. She shivered as she felt her blood run cold.

The man stood up and leaned forward, putting his face directly in front of Alice's. 'Darkness is coming,' he intoned, his voice hollow and haunting like a strong wind echoing through a deep cave. Alice tried to scream, but she made no noise, and she felt completely paralysed. The rest of the carriage seemed utterly oblivious to the man now leering so ominously close to her. With another silent scream, Alice tried to kick the man away from her.

She awoke with a jolt and her legs kicked out involuntarily. Her head was throbbing with a pain worse than before, and she looked around the carriage nervously. It was perfectly well lit, still filled with men in suits reading newspapers, but there was no sign of her nightmarish vision. The man sat opposite her was just an elderly gentleman reading the newspaper through his bifocals, and he most certainly had proper, human eyes. She gazed out of the window as she wound down from the nightmare, trying to calm herself.

'The next station is Oxford Circus,' announced the automated service, and Alice briefly toyed with the idea of just staying on the underground until the end of the line, but she couldn't really afford to take the day off, especially not on a whim. She'd already been given a written warning for taking two sick days, and management had told her that a third would result in non-specific 'disciplinary action.' Begrudgingly, Alice stood up and made her way to the carriage doors, off to face another tedious day.

CHAPTER III

'What time do you call this?' Asked a particularly stern-faced woman in an ill-fitting polyester shirt. She tapped her watch admonishingly, eyes fixed on Alice with an unwavering glare.

'One o'clock,' Alice said, looking at her manager with utter confusion.

'It's actually a minute past one. And what time does your shift start?' Jan, the store's manager, asked flatly. She wore the face of a middle school teacher about to administer detention.

'One o'clock?'

'Try to be on time for your shift, Alice. That's a minute we're paying you for that you haven't worked,' Jan said. She stared at Alice with eyes that seemed to bore into her soul as if waiting for an apology. Alice said nothing. *What do you want me to do, pay you back the 10p of overpay I'll 'earn' from that minute?!* It was bad enough she was still feeling a little hungover, plus the headaches and disturbing dreams, she really wasn't in the mood for this.

'Right, well,' Jan said conclusively, 'I need to meet with the Regents Marketing Group about this month's figures. You're on the till.' With that, she walked off in the direction of the staff room. Alice watched as she left before turning to the till, bottling up her thoughts and settling in for the long wait for the day to come to an end.

'Good afternoon, madam, how are you?' She greeted. 'Sorry, I'll just be one minute, sir.' She said. 'Would you be interested in registering for our new credit card service?' She asked. 'Your receipt's in the bag.' She stated. 'Thank you, have a good evening.' She smiled.

By the time Alice's break came around four hours later, she was ready to leave. She tried to tell herself it wasn't that much longer to go, but it didn't help. She was tired, she could feel her face turning paler by the second, her feet ached from standing, and if she had to smile politely again while a customer insulted her, she might go mad. The minute five o'clock came around, she removed her name badge and took herself off of the shop floor. She didn't want to spend another second there if she didn't have to.

Up until then, she'd tidied the display tables, served queues of customers during the store's busiest hour that day (possibly even that month), and held people up on several occasions when the till decided to chew up the receipt or, in her haste to serve everyone as quickly as possible, Alice had forgotten to take the customer's change out of the cash draw and had to wait for a manager to come and unlock it for her. The customers took it as a personal insult that she forgot to give them their change, and after much fiddling with the printer the till suddenly sprayed twenty different gift receipts.

Today was most certainly not Alice's day.

Pushing the door to the staff café open, Alice slowly walked in. She was relieved to discover that the place was entirely empty, the only noise coming from the television as the news was broadcast to an empty room. Alice felt exhausted, drained of all life, and it was a blessing she could enjoy her break without having to make small talk with any of her colleagues. She pushed the large button which read 'coffee' on the drinks machine, placing a polystyrene cup beneath the nozzle. The machine spluttered a murky brown liquid, the whole unit convulsing as if it were choking on its dying breath. Alice stood patiently, watching the machine as it struggled through its death-throes, coughing up the last of its life fluids before falling into silence.

She took the steaming cup of not-quite-coffee and tentatively took a sip, instantly regretting it. She scolded the roof of her mouth on the boiling soapy water which barely passed as a drink, and for legal reasons really shouldn't have been labelled 'coffee.' At least it was better than the dishwater they called 'tea.' She thought she heard someone come through the door and stand behind her, presumably waiting for the machine, but when she turned around to smile politely there was no-one else there. She took another sip of the unpleasant brown liquid, grimaced, and tipped the remainder of the drink down the drain, opting for a bottle of mineral water instead.

She crashed into an armchair facing the TV, letting herself sink into the cushioned seat (despite the crumbs and anonymous stains covering it), and took a gulp of water. It was icy cold and hurt her teeth, but it was refreshing after working on the dry shop floor for so long. She watched the news for a little while with only a fleeting interest. Politicians talked an awful lot but managed to say nothing, there was heavy traffic on the M25, and someone had been found dead in their home in Brentford. Then the news cut away to a man standing in front of a map of the UK while he droned on about winter being cold, cloudy and wet. CGI clouds with frowny faces swirled over London. It looked like they were in for heavy rain in Islington that weekend, as well as an influx of disgruntled cartoon clouds.

'And we have a large mass of clouds coming in from the south-west this evening, bringing heavy rain and storms through Saturday and Sunday. It looks like darkness is coming this weekend,' said Tom the Weatherman, his hands gesticulating like a marionette. Alice's head snapped up as she heard this, and stared, transfixed, at the screen. The image flickered unsettlingly, distortions running up and down the TV screen and cutting in and out. She stood up to fiddle with the aerial, but it was plugged in securely when she tried it. Her head began to ache, and she told herself it was just from her fatigue and watching the screen flash and go in and out of focus. 'Have a good evening,' said

Tom the Weatherman, and Alice jabbed at the power button. The image faded to black.

With a final gulp of the water, she chucked the bottle into the recycling bin, and steeled herself for the remaining few hours of work.

The day carried on in much the same way it had started, and by the time the end of her shift came, Alice couldn't have clocked out any quicker if she'd tried. Her head was now pounding, like someone was hammering nails inside her skull, and she figured she was just getting too stressed out, especially since she'd been deprived of a decent cup of tea or coffee for the past eight hours. Tired, stressed, and wondering if she was experiencing the onset of an aneurysm, Alice brushed her staff card against the door lock, beeped, and headed straight for home. She couldn't wait to get in, chill out and settle down for a lazy night in with Rachel.

By the time she'd alighted at Highbury and Islington, Alice was clearly fatigued and her eyes were starting to play tricks on her. In the twilight of the evening, even the most mundane of things seemed to hide some dark secret. Her walk home was plagued by these evil illusions, as shadows cast by piled up bins seemed to hide hideous, hulking monstrosities, and unearthly things appeared to lurk in every corner and alleyway. However, whenever Alice turned to see what these things were, they would promptly vanish or shape-shift into an innocent shadow, and she'd console herself that it was likely just an illusion caused by her impending migraine. It reminded her of when she was eight or nine, and come bedtime she'd see nothing but monsters; lurking in her cupboard, hiding under her bed, waiting at the end of the hallway... She didn't have her imaginary friend to chase away the shadows tonight, though.

She opened the door to her building – a row of old town-houses that had been knocked through and converted to accommodate a number of basic studios and apartments – and she headed up the stairs towards their flat on the second floor. The place was dimly lit at the best of times, but evidently a fuse had blown again and taken out all of the lighting on her floor. Not that it really mattered, as a glimmer of street-light shone through the window at the end of the corridor, faintly illuminating the way. They'd just light a couple of candles or use the lights on their phones for tonight, and wait for the landlord to fix the fuse.

Alice was fumbling around in the dim light of the corridor, looking for her keys, when from behind her she heard a low, guttural rumble. *'Darkness is coming.'*

She whirled around, and was greeted by a tall, dark figure. Again, she recognised the hooded figure with its sinister leer, those dark soulless eyes seemingly draining the light from the world. She froze in terror, trapped and helpless against this thing that seemed to constantly haunt her, and tried to convince herself it was only a stress-induced hallucination. Out of the corner of her eye she saw something moving at the end of the corridor. She looked up, and stood in the faint orange glow from the street outside she could see the silhouette of a familiar shape, the figure of the man in the coat and hat. His long coat swayed from side to side as he made his way towards her, and in that instance Alice realised with horror that her nightmare from Halloween had not been a dream.

She crumpled to the floor, closing her eyes tightly and willing this all to be some horrible dream, begging to wake up and find out it was Friday morning again, but the man/creature/thing continued to bear down on her. She remembered the thoughts of the monsters she'd imagined as a child, trying to convince herself that none of this was real, but as she tried to push it away, more and more images were conjured up in her imagination. She found herself back on that street on Halloween, where this had all began. She could hear shouting, a familiar voice which sounded as if it was from some distant memory or half-remembered dream, but she couldn't hear what it was saying. There was a hiss, a growl, and the inexplicable crackling of electricity, and she suddenly felt two hands clasp either side of her head.

Panic truly overcame Alice, and she was certain that this was either the end or that she would need to be committed to a psychiatric ward. She tried to open her eyes, but all she could see was darkness. Oily shadows swam in front of her mind's eye, swirling around like a swarm of eels. She could faintly hear whispers coming from the liquid shadows. The darkness enveloped her, surrounding Alice's entire being, caressing her body like the ebb and flow of the ocean. She was adrift in an endless black sea, and she could feel herself being taken away by the current.

CHAPTER IV

The next thing Alice knew, she was waking up in the flat. Her head throbbed with an agonising headache that extended from her forehead, down through her teeth and into her neck. Her vision was blurred and blotchy, as if she'd been staring at the sun for too long. She was sprawled out unceremoniously on the sofa, one of the throw cushions propping her head up. The lights were back on. Swinging her legs around, she tried to stand up, but paused mid-motion to stop her head spinning. *Bloody hell, what a dream*, she thought as she regained her balance. She felt like she had a horrendous hangover, but at least it had all been just a dr-

'Hey, hey, hey! Not so fast. Take it easy,' a voice said from somewhere behind her. She craned her neck, which made a disconcerting noise like crumpling paper, to see who was speaking to her. She felt a sinking feeling in the pit of her stomach as reality started to dawn on her again.

'What the hell do you think you're doing?!'

Alice screamed, leaping to her feet with fury, and immediately regretted it as her head threatened to explode.

The kitchen looked as if a bomb had gone off. The cupboards had been emptied, their contents scattered across the counter tops. The bins had been upended, rubbish strewn across the floor. The fridge stood with it's door lazily hanging open. At the heart of the debris, and presumably the catalyst of this chaos, was the man in the coat and hat. He was knelt down amongst the contents of the bin, but stood up when Alice shouted at him. He dropped a torn-up page of the Guardian. *Oh god, it hadn't all been a damn dream.*

'Have you received anything unusual lately? Strange gift, unexpected letter, something out of the ordinary? Weird artefacts which give you a lingering sense of dread?' He asked, completely ignoring the visible rage, fear, confusion and myriad other emotions etched on his unwitting host's face, and clearly oblivious that breaking and entering – and rummaging through someone's bin – is unacceptable behaviour in civilised society.

'What? No! Who are you and what are you doing in my kitchen?' Alice asked furiously, mixed with the panic of having a complete stranger pillaging her kitchen, and she felt as if her eyeballs were about to pop out of their sockets. 'What are you doing *to* my kitchen?!'

'Sorry, I don't believe I've formally introduced myself yet. Terrible manners. I'm Sam. Sam Hain.' The man took a few steps forward, kicking aside empty bottles and packets as he went, and extended a hand towards her, but Alice refused to shake it.

'Like the Pagan festival?' She asked indignantly.

'As a matter of fact, I do, although that's pronounced 'sah-win," Sam replied helpfully. Alice didn't care. She simply stood the other side of the sofa from her unwelcome guest, uncertain as to what to do. She eyed the house phone, off of its base unit and laying on one of the kitchen counters. Her mobile wasn't in her pockets. If she wanted to call for help, she'd just have to make a run for it. She span on her heels, and made a dash for the door.

It was locked.

In her panic, she fumbled with the lock, trying desperately to open the door, but she wasn't able to release the catch on the handle fast enough. The man who called himself Sam Hain was stood right behind her. He lifted his hands to hold her by the shoulders, but he left them hovering.

'Please, don't panic. I'm not an intruder – well, I suppose I sort of am – but I certainly don't mean you any harm,' Sam spoke softly, trying to calm her down. She didn't trust his calmness, and turned around as she pushed herself back against the door.

'So what, precisely, do you think you're doing in my home?' Alice spat through gritted teeth.

'You've been having piercing headaches, sometimes with disturbing visions. Like a nightmare you can't quite wake up from. Am I right?' He slowly took a step back, allowing her some space. Tentatively, she nodded.

'That's why I'm here, Alice. I'm one of the few people who knows about the things you're experiencing.'

'How do you know my name?' Alice asked, her voice quivering more with worry than with anger now.

'You really shouldn't throw out your old bank statements, you know. Don't you keep account of your finances?' Sam sat down on the sofa, and gestured for Alice to take a seat. 'That's not why I'm here, though. I'm here because of what happened last night, and what's been happening since.'

She was still unsure about the situation, but Alice got the sense that this man really didn't mean her any harm, even if he had completely trashed her kitchen. Cautiously, she took a seat in the armchair nearest the door. She was shaking inside, and wished Rachel would get back home soon. *Where the hell is she?*

'So what do you know about my 'visions?'' Alice asked.

'More than you'd probably think,' Sam answered, and he removed his hat, ruffling his flattened hair. 'I deal with the... extraordinary. Last night, I was on a case. There was something here that shouldn't have been, and I had to do something about it.'

'That man that you started fighting?' Alice asked, wondering where this was going.

'Yes. Although he wasn't so much a man as a thing shaped like a man. He was an entity from another dimension, causing trouble where he shouldn't.'

Alice eyed him incredulously. 'Of course. So you're a demon hunter? Right? Am I supposed to believe that?'

'Well, not really a demon-hunter, although that is part of the job description. I'm an occult detective. I deal with cases involving the esoteric and the supernatural.' The man who called himself Sam Hain spoke with such conviction that Alice almost believed him.

'All right then. Supernatural sleuth. Gotcha. Forgot to take your pills this morning?' She retorted sarcastically. Again she considered making a move for the phone, but rather than calling the police she was now thinking about getting in touch with Bedlam to let them know they were missing a patient.

"Darkness is coming.' Am I right?' Sam asked casually, watching Alice closely for any kind of reaction.

She felt time come to a standstill, and she could see a knowing look behind the strange man's eyes. It was as if his words had suddenly made it all the more real. *How could he have known?* Her voice lowered to almost a whisper. 'Yeah. Something like that.'

Sam stood up and made his way over to the window. He gazed out, overlooking a terrace of houses, beyond which the tiny pin-pricks of light from the rest of the city could be seen. He clasped his hands behind his back pensively. 'I've been following the signs for some time now. 'Darkness is coming,' they warned. Forces beyond our reckoning are stirring in the Void, trying to breach the walls between our world and their own. I'm trying to get to the bottom of what's going on, and – for whatever reason – on All Hallows' Eve, things have been converging on you, Alice.'

Alice sat in silence for a while, her mind elsewhere. She thought of the man in the hood, of running in fear and of the niggling sensation at the back of her mind that something sinister was going on. 'Why me?' She eventually asked, her voice quiet and uncertain.

'May I?' Sam asked, returning to sit opposite Alice. He raised his hands towards her head, and she jerked backwards, eyeing him suspiciously.

'What are you doing?'

'I'm going to take a peek inside your mind,' he said, and he saw the look of concern written across Alice's face. 'Don't worry,' he added, 'I won't see anything you don't want me to see, only the things I need. But I need your consent, if you'll allow me?'

Alice nodded silently as she allowed Sam's hands to gently hold either side of her head. She felt his forefingers against her temples, the tips of his fingers resting by the sides of her eyes, and she felt the pain in her head begin to fade. It ebbed and flowed like the coming and going of the tide, the headache gradually waning. First, the pain receded from her teeth. Then her forehead stopped throbbing, and she could feel the ache shrink towards the back of her head.

'Very clever... They must really like you,' Sam muttered, 'unfortunately for them, I'm clever-er.'

Like water draining down a plug hole, Alice felt the pounding headache swirl out of the back of her head. It was as if a great weight had been lifted from her. She opened her eyes, and the world looked like she was seeing it all for the first time. Sam merely grinned at her and said, 'how's your headache now?'

Alice blinked slightly in confusion. Her headache was gone entirely. No remnant of the migraine remained, not even a vague tingling in her teeth. She didn't even feel anxious or panicked. Apparently her look of confusion and realisation was fairly evident, as Sam gave a knowing chuckle.

'How did you do that?' She eventually asked.

'Quite simply,' Sam stated matter-of-factly.

'It's gone completely.'

'When I first bumped into you, I was tracking a rift, a rip in the walls between our world and another,' Sam began to explain. 'Around Halloween, the veil between dimensions is at its thinnest, allowing for easier interactions between different dimensions, even to cross from one world to another as easily as walking into a different room – if you know how to open the door. That entity seized the opportunity to come into our realm of existence, taking on the form of a man. Why? I don't know. Maybe the foothold for the coming Darkness... Some of its essence imprinted on you. Something drew it to you, and when I tried to banish it back to the Void, a part of it was left behind. Like a metaphysical bee sting,' Sam paused, and with a sideways smile he added, 'nice costume, by the way.'

'You mean a part of that thing was in me?!' Alice exclaimed. 'That's what was causing the headaches and the nightmares?'

'In a manner of speaking, yes. That's why it seemed to still haunt you. But I've removed its essence from your mind, you should sleep soundly tonight.'

Alice nodded, a little dumbstruck by what she was hearing. 'You know this sounds like a very flimsy plot for a fantasy horror story, don't you?' She mocked, but from the little time she'd spent getting to know Sam and what she'd experienced, it was strangely starting to sound more and more plausible. A few days ago, she was a normal girl in her twenties, going about a perfectly normal life. Now she'd somehow found herself in a world of demons and monsters. 'Again, why me?'

'I wish I could say that you just happened to be in the wrong place at the wrong time. I really do. And to be honest, that is a large part of what's brought me here. But there's something special about you, Alice. You have a gift not many people have. I saw it in you last night, and I see it in you now,' he said, and he sounded almost sorry for her. 'Let me ask you something, when you were growing up, did you ever believe in monsters under your bed? Hiding in your wardrobe?'

Alice nodded. 'I used to think I could see monsters lurking in the shadows of my bedroom, when I was about nine. Sometimes they appeared to be so real... My mum kept trying to tell me that it was all in my head, and it was nothing to be scared of.'

'Well, it's not your mother's fault for not knowing. Not a lot of people do, not really,' he said. 'There are things which exist in the places beyond this world. Things from other realms, other dimensions. They weren't just in your head, Alice, you didn't imagine them... The monsters beneath your bed were real. As were your imaginary friends. You've been given the soul-sight, the ability to see things which others don't, and to distinguish the light and the dark. Whether this is a blessing or a curse is up to you.' He spoke in a tone not unlike an adult telling a child about the dangers of playing with fire. A shiver ran up Alice's spine.

'You're serious, aren't you?' She asked, and she already knew that what Sam was saying was the truth. 'You're really, properly serious...'

'I don't joke around with things like this,' he replied, his face like stone, 'not very often, anyway.'

'So, that thing... It doesn't feel like it's in my head any more, and I can't see it. It's finally gone?'

'Oh no, quite the contrary. It's still here, somewhere,' Sam said with a dismissive wave of his hand, 'I just removed its hold on your mind. But now that its link to you is severed, I doubt it's going to be very happy...'

As if on cue, there was a sudden, ear-piercing scream from outside. 'That'll be for us then,' Sam said with a grin, and in one swift motion he jumped up, threw on his hat, unlocked the door and sprinted off down the corridor. Alice started after him, running along the corridor and down the stairs only a few steps behind, being careful not to step on Sam's coat as it billowed out behind him. They heard another terrified scream coming from the street, and Sam jumped the last few steps and barged through the front door. As Alice followed, she could see the light from the street lights flickering on the pavement just outside of the door.

In the middle of the street stood Rachel, two pizza boxes balanced in her arms with a plastic bag slung around her wrist, and a man, a hood pulled low, partially concealing his face, walking slowly towards her. He moved in an eerie, inhuman manner, his body twitching erratically, and his hollow eyes were as black as the night. Alice's heart dropped. The unearthly being staggered towards Rachel with its uneven gait. Occasionally it would appear to crack, like old plaster peeling away. The street lights flickered on and off as the creature approached, and each light it passed would immediately extinguish. The road behind it was completely dark, the light of every home and lamp post now dead.

'That's-'

'The thing from your nightmares? Yes, I know. Persistent bugger,' Sam whispered, and reached into his pocket, drawing out something which looked like a wand, although it was made from a chrome-like metal with a pointed clear crystal at its front and a shiny black stone at the end. Putting on a pair of circular sunglasses, he raised the metal wand and pointed it towards the hooded entity. 'Someone's clearly not very happy I broke its hold on you!'

Rachel remained stood in the middle of the road, frozen in fear as the thing approached her. She no longer screamed, she just stared directly at the man in the hood with her mouth agape. The inexplicable shadow emanating from the man stretched out, causing the remaining street lights to go out, and an unnatural darkness descended upon them all. Wordlessly, Rachel dropped the pizza boxes to the floor.

'Hey, you! Person!' Sam shouted towards the inanimate woman in the road.

'Rachel,' Alice said helpfully.

'Rachel! I'd step away from the being of unimaginable darkness if I was you,' he said, but she didn't seem to hear him.

Taking a couple of steps forward, Sam addressed the creature. 'You know you don't belong here,' he declared, and the being in the hood stopped. It remained stock still in the middle of the road, a few paces from Rachel. Its body convulsed and juddered, and it hissed viciously at Sam. 'I sent you back to the Void, and you just came crawling back. But your power is fading, and try as you might you can feel your grip on this plane weakening. Now, you can either do the sensible thing and go grovelling back to your Dark Masters, or you can try your luck with me.'

The creature leered forwards and hissed in defiance. It began to stagger towards Rachel again, and wisps of shadow reached out to her.

'Oh, suit your-bloody-self' Sam said, almost wearily, and he raised his wand, pointing it at the creature. 'Being of Darkness, Devourer of Light, I banish thee back to the Void from whence thee came!'

The creature writhed uncomfortably as Sam spoke, hissing and spitting at him. But nothing happened. The darkness continued to spread, unabated by Sam's magick, and tentacle-like shadows lapped at Rachel's feet, coiling around and around, until one latched onto her ankle. The creature seemed to have her completely paralysed. Sam spun on his heel and faced Alice.

'Alice, this thing has a foothold on this world and, like it or not, it used you as an anchor. When it left a part of itself in your mind, it was like a foot in the interdimensional door. I need you to be one-hundred percent focused.'

Alice felt fear grip her once again and she tried to look him in the eyes, but couldn't see through the dark lenses of the circular glasses. She nodded uncertainly to him.

'Good. Now, I need you to cast this demon to Hell.'

'What? How do I-? What?!' Alice stammered. She glanced over towards the entity, the body of the hooded man now swathed in darkness, a shadowy form of something far more sinister and foreboding looming large behind him.

'My will alone can't banish this thing. It used your mind to bring itself into this world, and your mind can send it back.'

Alice steeled herself for the worst. Twenty-four hours ago, she had been at a Halloween costume party, forgetting about the stress of day-to-day reality and having a good time. Now what had once been the day-to-day seemed like a distant memory, and considerably more relaxing. She would've been afraid, but fear no longer seemed like a strong enough emotion to describe what she was feeling. She could feel her body turning numb, almost like she was going to pass out, and a solid lump was wedged in her throat and chest. It was like being called up in front of the class to do a presentation in primary school, but a thousand times worse and involved shadow demons from another dimension. She glanced back at Sam, her eyes watering. He simply nodded to her.

'I banish thee to the void from whence thee came,' Alice said, her voice wavering uncertainly. She was about ready to crumble and collapse to the floor. The creature in the man in the hood snapped its head at an unnatural angle to face her, and she froze in place. *I can't do this*, she thought, *why the hell am I even in this mess? I don't- I can't-*

'Believe in the words you're saying, Alice,' Sam

said, 'believe you have the power to send this thing back to the Void! Nine-tenths of magick is intent. A spell is nothing but empty words if you don't believe in it.' Sam held his hand out to her, and smiled gently. 'Take my hand, we'll do this together.'

Something about the man called Sam Hain was peculiarly calming. Maybe it was something about the way he spoke, she didn't know, but Alice felt her nerves slowly begin to settle. Hesitantly, she took hold of Sam's hand, and felt his grip tighten.

'Now let's send this bugger back to the shadows, hey? Let's show them not to mess with Sam and Alice!'

'We banish thee to the Void from whence thee came!' They shouted in unison, and Alice felt an energy course through her veins. It felt as if her entire being was being enveloped in some kind of etheric energy, and for a brief moment seemed to meld into Sam too. Then she noticed the crystal point beginning to glow.

A bolt of violet energy burst from the front of the wand and struck the entity squarely in the chest. The thing that looked like a man began to convulse, its body shook violently, and a dazzling purple light burst from its eyes and mouth as it screamed an unearthly scream. Its limbs wobbled uselessly at its sides. There was a sudden flash of blinding light which forced Alice and Rachel to cover their eyes. When they were able to look again, the figure of a man had disappeared, and where it had once stood only a pair of shoes remained. All of the lights down the street came back on.

'What just happened?' Rachel asked, her voice wavering and a look of fear mixed with confusion on her face.

'Halloween trick,' Sam said nonchalantly without missing a beat. He removed the sunglasses and put them back inside his coat's pocket, along with the thing which resembled a wand. 'Good, isn't it?'

'B-but, the smouldering shoes? The, the-'

'Amateur theatrics. Not as good as some of the stuff they can do on the West End, but this has been our best trick yet. Wouldn't you say, Alice?' He nudged her with his elbow as he said this, and tilted his head towards her.

'Oh, yeah. Yes. Definitely,' Alice stammered uncertainly. Everything she'd experienced had finally caught up with her, and she was feeling more than a little overwhelmed by it all. Despite everything she'd just witnessed, this seemed to be a good enough explanation for Rachel. She knelt down to pick up the pizza boxes and made her way towards the door to the flat.

'If these pizzas are ruined because of your little trick, you're paying for them, mister!' She shouted before disappearing into the building.

'You know, I really didn't think she'd buy that,' Alice said, looking up at Sam.

'Nor did I...'

They both stood in silence for a little while,

staring at the pair of shoes which now sat in the middle of the road in Islington, a few faint wisps of smoke still drifting from them. The night was still and serenely quiet, and for the first time in what felt like forever, Alice didn't have a sense of dread hanging over her.

'The Earth plane is shifting again. In a few hours, the divide between this world and the next won't be quite as thin,' Sam said, standing with his head towards the sky, as if he could feel the change in the wind. 'You can feel it too, can't you.'

'This is all so... Insane,' Alice said to him. Sam simply nodded.

'I understand, it's a bit much to take in all at once. When you've had some time to process this, or if you ever need anything, here's my card.' He handed her a business card. It was black with golden text, and a pentagram in its centre.

Sam Hain
Occult Detective
Divination – Evocation
Astral Projection – Magickal Protection
www.SamHainsCasebook.co.uk

'If you do decide to venture down this particular rabbit hole, please get in touch. I could use someone with your skills. After all, the walls between worlds may be building back up, but things are never as normal as they appear.' He secured his hat firmly on his head, and with a final nod he bid her farewell. 'I have a feeling this won't be the last I'll be seeing of you, Alice Carroll. Until our paths cross again, take care.'

'You too,' Alice said with a bemused wave, and she watched as the strange man walked down the road, his coat billowing in the cold night wind. For the briefest of moments, she was sure she could see the glimmer of an aura around his figure, but in the blink of an eye it was gone. Although she couldn't quite explain everything, she felt like something important had happened to her. She turned and made her way back towards the door of the townhouse, and she cast one last glance over her shoulder towards Sam, but he was already gone, vanished into the night.

She stood for quite some time, staring down the street and out into the night, lost in her thoughts.

'Do you want your pizza or what?' She could hear Rachel calling out to her from the second-floor window.

'Just coming,' Alice shouted back, looking up at the window with a wave. She skipped over the doorstep, closed the door, and walked back up the stairs towards the flat. It was perfectly, reassuringly normal inside. The lights cast a warm glow over the room, where Rachel was sat on the sofa flicking through the channels on the TV. The smell of fresh takeaway pizza and chips filled the air.

'Fancy a drink?' Alice asked as she flung her coat over the back of the sofa.

'Yeah, please, cider's in the fridge,' Rachel said. She must have bought the whole Halloween trick thing, because she didn't seem to have a care in the world. 'What do you want to watch?'

'I don't know, what's on?'

Rachel began to reel off the exhaustive list on the TV guide, but Alice didn't hear a word of what she was saying. She stood in the entrance to the kitchen, dumbstruck, faced with the horror that awaited her. The contents of the bins, strewn across the room from Sam's haphazard investigation, still lay in the state of chaos he'd left them in.

That bastard.

ABOUT THE AUTHOR

Bron James is an author of science fiction, fantasy and magical realism. He was born with a silver pen in his mouth and has been making up stories for as long as he can remember. His professional début work of fiction, the first instalment of the *Sam Hain* series of novellas, was first published in 2013.

Born and raised in the south of England, Bron presently lives in London where he writes stories, drinks tea, and dreams improbable dreams.

~

www.bronjames.co.uk

More Titles in the *Sam Hain* Series

Volume I
All Hallows' Eve
A Night in Knightsbridge
The Grimditch Butcher
The Regents
The Eye of the Oracle
Convergence

~

www.samhainscasebook.co.uk